Jenny Jungle

Janey Levy

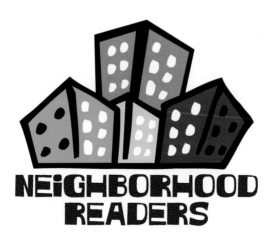

NEIGHBORHOOD READERS

Rosen Classroom Books & Materials™

New York

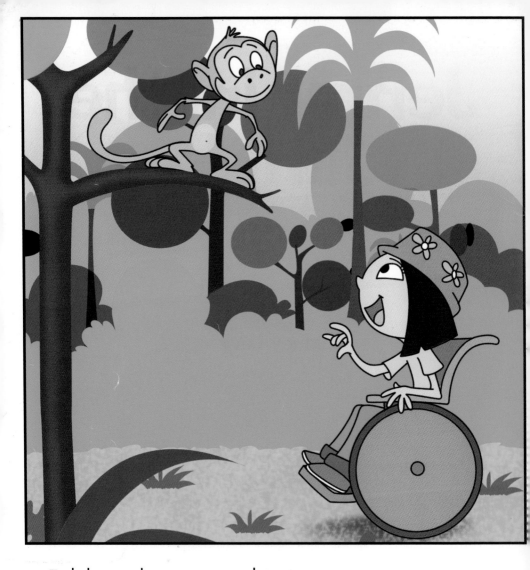

I like the monkey.

2

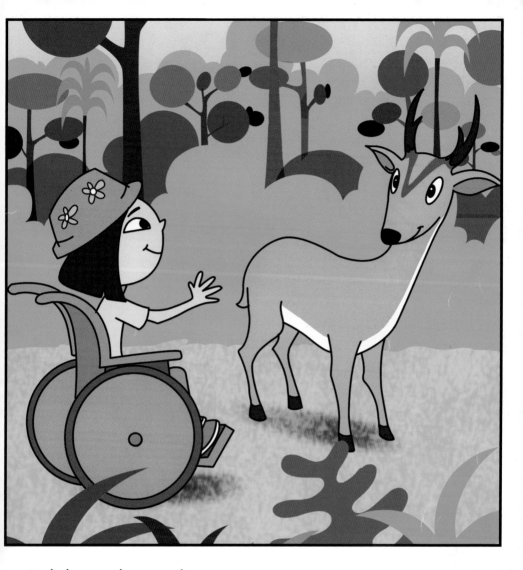

I like the deer.

3

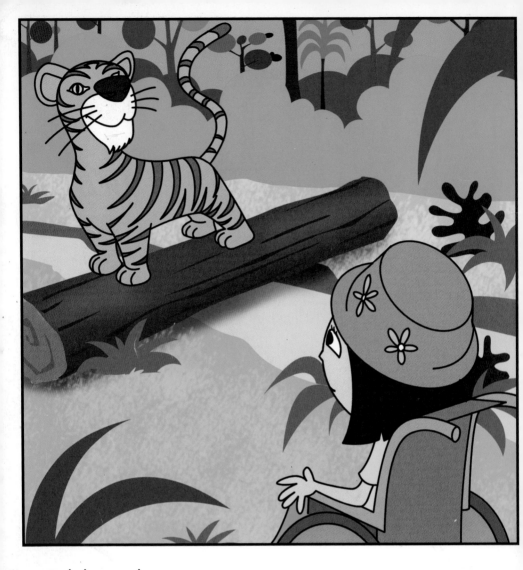

I like the tiger.

4

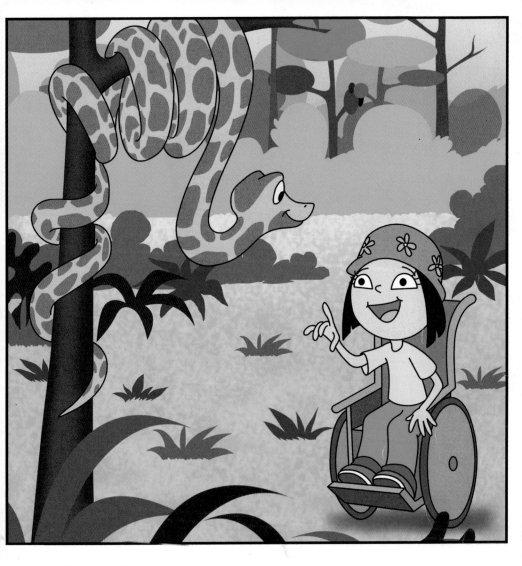

I like the snake.

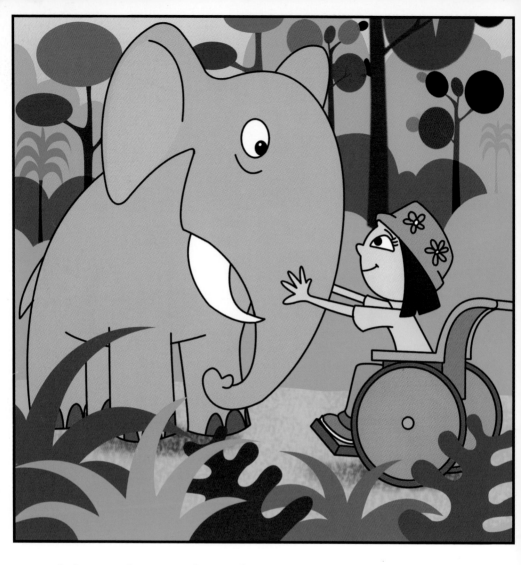

I like the elephant.

6

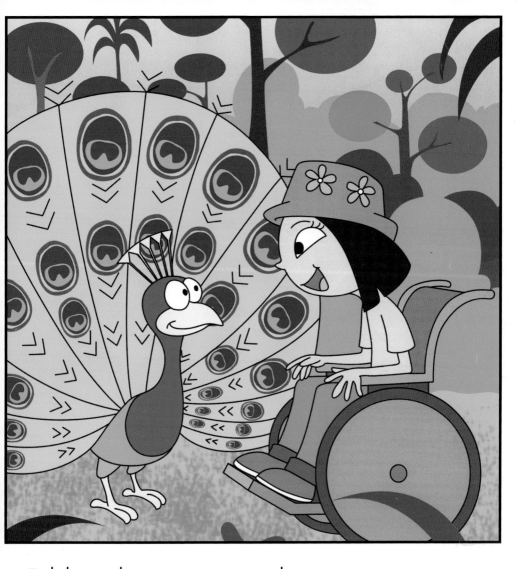

I like the peacock.

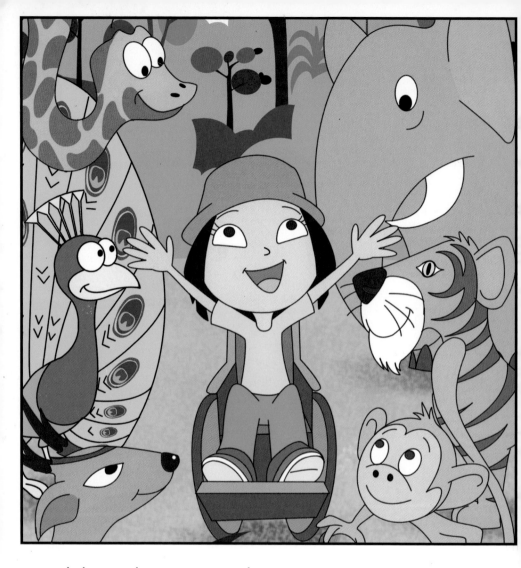

I like the jungle!

8